# Contents

# The *fairy* world

The Superfairies of Peaseblossom Woods use teamwork to rescue animals in trouble. They bring together their special superskills, petal power and lots of love.

## Superfairy Rose

can blow super healing fairy kisses to make the animals in Peaseblossom Woods feel better.

# The Copper Queen

by Janey Louise Jones
illustrated by Jennie Poh

Curious Fox
a capstone company-publishers for children

First published in 2018 by Curious Fox, an imprint of Capstone Global Library Limited, 264 Banbury Road, Oxford, OX2 7DY – Registered company number: 6695582

www.curious-fox.com


All characters in this publication are fictitious and any resemblance to real persons, living or dead, is purely coincidental.

ISBN 978 1 78202 809 3
21 20 19 18 17
10 9 8 7 6 5 4 3 2 1

A CIP catalogue for this book is available from the British Library.





Printed and bound in India.

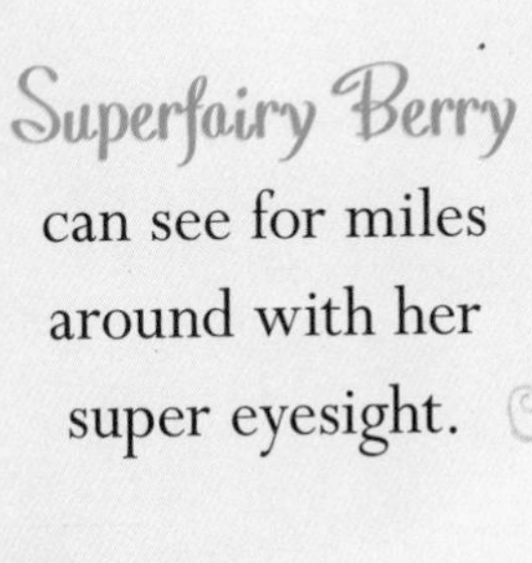

## Superfairy Berry

can see for miles
around with her
super eyesight.

## Superfairy Star

can create super dazzling
brightness in one dainty spin
to lighten up dark places.

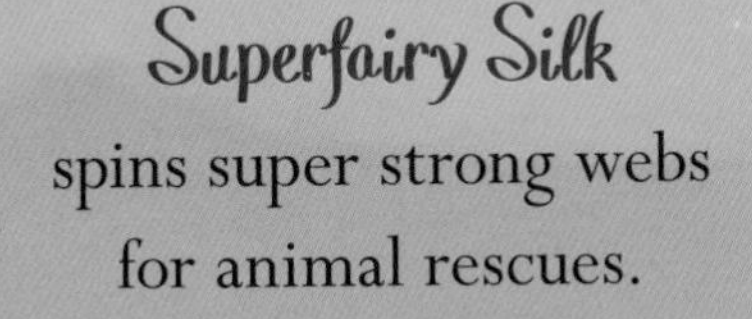

## Superfairy Silk

spins super strong webs
for animal rescues.

# Chapter 1

## Falling leaves

The leaves on the trees in Peaseblossom Woods turned slowly from deepest green to shimmering shades of gold, bronze and copper.

At first, one or two leaves dropped from the branches and floated through the woods to the ground below.

Then a handful of leaves fell.

Soon more followed.

After that, all the autumn leaves began to flutter down from the trees.

Fall . . .

Falling . . .

Fallen.

The branches became bare, and a crisp blanket of golden leaves carpeted the woodland floor.

Inside the cherry blossom tree, the Superfairies were getting ready for the arrival of autumn and the Copper Queen.

"Not long until the Copper Queen's Masked Dance through the woods!" said Superfairy Berry. "Let's make our masks today!"

"I love the Masked Dance!" said Star. "It's so thrilling to see the beautiful Copper Queen, and dressing up is great fun. Not to mention the dancing! You all know I love to dance."

Star did a twirl, but then, for a moment, she lost her smile. "But, *why* must the trees lose all the pretty leaves?" she asked.

"It's getting too cold and windy for them now," said Rose. "And the trees need to prepare for the big winter sleep so that they can *burst* to life again next spring! We can't expect them to go on and on, bearing leaves and blossoms and berries without a rest now, can we?"

"I suppose that's true," said Star.

"Plus it's fun to *crunch* in the leaves in autumn!" Berry added. "And there are always dressing-up parties this time of year. And festivals and feasts too. I love it!"

"Crunching through leaves is super fun!" Star agreed, brightening up a little.

"Think of it this way," said Rose. "Every season is so beautiful because it's unique.

They're all part of a perfect pattern for the whole year. There are so many delicious berries and fruits ripening now. We can make some jams to enjoy in winter!"

"And in spring, there are snowdrops and daffodils to admire!" said Silk.

"I love the warm sun and ripe strawberries in summer!" said Berry.

Star was happy with these thoughts and danced through to the kitchen to start making some plum jam for the feast. They would all be hungry after the Masked Dance.

Out in the woods, the young animals collected decorations for their masks.

"I can't wait to wear a mask at the dance!" said Susie Squirrel. "And see the Copper Queen for the first time."

"Me too!" agreed Martha Mouse.

They had heard all about the beautiful Copper Queen and were excited to see her. It would be such fun playing hide-and-seek behind their masks at the dance!

"It's as if the whole world has turned to gold!" squealed Violet the Velvet Rabbit. "Granny told me this would happen, but I've never seen it before!

Everything is so beautiful! I've even found some gold leaves for my mask."

"And I've found some cool sycamore helicopters!" Susie Squirrel said.

"Look! These pretty feathers will look great on my mask. Ooh, they're tickly." Dancer the Wild Pony giggled.

"Wow! I love these blackberry lilies!" exclaimed Cloud, Dancer's sister. "We're going to look so lovely!"

Basil Bear, Sonny Squirrel and Billy Badger had already finished making their masks. They wanted to play now. They moved to a wider part of the woods, near the meadow.

Basil had made a ball by rolling grasses and moss tightly together.

"Okay, you can be in goal, Billy!" shouted Basil. "And, Sonny, I'll be the striker. You pass the ball to me. Got that?"

At first, Billy and Sonny did as they were told.

"This way!" called Basil.

"Pass to me!" Basil yelled.

"Faster!" shouted Basil.

"My ball!" Basil insisted.

"That *was* a goal!" Basil complained.

Basil chased after the ball as it rolled towards the river. Billy and Sonny huddled together.

"Is it just me, or is Basil being super bossy today?" said Billy.

"It's not just you. I think that too!" agreed Sonny.

The boys tried to make the game more equal. They called out some instructions to Basil.

"Basil, you pass it to me!" called Sonny.

"Yeah, this way!" said Billy. "And it's your turn to be goalie."

Basil ignored his friends. As far as he was concerned, it was his ball, his rules.

Finally, Billy snapped.

"Stop bossing us around, Basil. This isn't fun!" said Billy.

"Yeah," agreed Sonny. "You're way too bossy. We want to have a turn with the ball. You're not being fair to us! It's not all about you."

"It's not about taking turns," said Basil. "It's about who is best!"

"Best at giving orders!" said Sonny.

"If you're going to be spoilsports, I'll take my ball and play somewhere else!" said Basil, sounding huffy.

Picking up the ball, he set off on his own. "Good luck without a ball!" Basil called over his shoulder.

Once Basil was out of sight, Billy turned to Sonny.

"Oooh, Basil is sooo annoying. Let's play a trick on him!" he said.

Sonny thought for a moment, trying to imagine what some of his bigger cousins might do. "Let's hide from him, then call his name!"

"Hee-hee," laughed Billy gleefully. "Great idea!"

Sonny looked around. "We should both hide in different places. Then we'll call and whistle at the same time. Basil won't be able to work out which direction it's coming from."

"Good thinking," said Billy. "I'll go behind this mound of earth over here . . ."

"And I'll climb that tree over there," said Sonny. "Try not to laugh when he gets close!"

"You're right!" agreed Billy. "That'll give it away. Do you think Basil will come back this way soon?"

"Well, he has to pass here to get home," said Sonny. "And, he really hates playing on his own . . ."

"Yes, because he doesn't like not having someone to boss around!" agreed Billy.

# Chapter 2

## Hide-and-seek

The boys got into their hiding positions. Billy crouched down low behind the mound. Sonny lay flat on his stomach on a wide branch.

Then they waited.

Basil kicked the ball here and there near the Mousey House. At first, he enjoyed playing on his own. But after a while, he became bored. He decided to head back to the spot where he'd left his friends.

Basil wandered back through the woods, whistling to himself and singing rhymes. Then he heard his name being called.

"Basil!" called Sonny from the tree branch.

"Basil! Where are you? We'd really like to play with you again!" called Billy from behind the mound.

Basil was glad to hear his friends' familiar voices, but he couldn't work out where they were coming from.

He looked to the left and the right. He looked in front and behind. He checked above and below. But he couldn't see his friends anywhere.

Sonny called again. "Basil!"

"Hey, where are you?" replied Basil.

"Here!" said Sonny, not giving away any information to help Basil.

"We're over here," Billy added. "Hurry up, we're having so much fun!"

"But I can't see you anywhere!" Basil complained. He was getting very frustrated.

A cold wind was starting to blow through the woods. Basil spun around, looking in every direction. He charged along the pathway and suddenly . . .

"Aaaarrrgh!" Basil screamed. "I'm f-a-l-l-i-n-g . . ."

He disappeared under some leaves.

Billy and Sonny peeked out from their hiding spots, trying to see what was going on. What had happened to Basil?

Billy rushed over to where Basil had disappeared. "He's fallen down a hole!" he shouted.

"Oh, no!" exclaimed Sonny. He quickly climbed down from the tree and joined Billy.

They expected Basil to climb angrily out of the hole.

But he did not.

A few moments passed. They peered down the dark hole.

"Basil? Are you okay?" called Sonny.

"We're here!" said Billy. "We'll help you!"

The boys felt bad about their friend falling. They prepared to lean into the hole to help him out.

Just at that moment, a fierce wind whipped through the woods.

*Whoosh!*

The wind was wild and strong. It picked up Sonny and Billy and carried them through the woods.

Leaves of copper, bronze and gold

flapped

flew

tossed

and

swirled

in every direction.

When the angry wind finally settled, Sonny and Billy were nowhere near where they had started.

"We need to go back and help Basil!" said Sonny.

The boys went back as quickly as they could to help Basil. Eventually they arrived back at the wide part of the woods near the meadow. There were leaves everywhere. The hole Basil had fallen into was nowhere to be seen.

"Basil! Basil! Where are you?" cried Sonny.

There was no reply.

Sonny went to look behind all the big trees.

Billy went down to the river to look.

There was no sign of him.

"Oh, dear," said Billy. "What if he's hurt in that hole, and now we can't find him?"

“We have to keep looking!” said Sonny. “You go that way. I’ll go this way. Call his name! We can meet back here in a few minutes.”

“Okay, good idea,” said Billy.

“Basil!”

“Oh, Basil!”

“Basil, where are you?”

“We’re sorry, Basil!”

The boys tried their best, but they simply couldn't find Basil and were frantic with worry.

There was only one thing to do. Sonny and Billy rang the bells for the Superfairies.

*Ting-a-ling-a-ling!*

Chapter 3

# Time to rescue

Over at the cherry blossom tree, the Superfairies heard the bells and sped into action.

"Forget the masks! The jam can wait! Let's get ready to rescue!" said Rose.

The Superfairies gathered all their rescue kits together, lifted their wands, and met in their fairycopter.

As Berry prepared for take-off, Rose looked at the Strawberry computer to see what the problem was.

"I can see Sonny and Billy. They look frantic with worry near the meadow," said Rose. "But there's a split screen.

Basil looks like he's trapped in a dark hole somewhere!"

"This sounds very worrying!" said Berry. "I'll get us there as fast as I can! Five, four, three, two, one . . . go, go, go!"

The Superfairies were soon in the air. Before long, the fairycopter landed next to Sonny and Billy.

"Thank goodness!" said Billy when he spotted the Superfairies. "We were playing hide-and-seek. Basil fell in a big hole. Then a big gust of wind whipped up all the leaves, and we were carried away. Now we can't find him. There are too many leaves for us to move them all."

"Oh, dear," said Rose. "Have you tried calling his name?"

"Yes, and no reply!" said Billy sadly. "We've looked everywhere."

"Let's start by flying across the whole area, calling his name," suggested Star.

The Superfairies tried that, but Basil still did not respond.

"There must be something else . . ." said Berry. "I know! Let's see if the Strawberry computer's heat-search system can pinpoint where he is!"

"Good thinking," said Rose. She took out the computer and pressed the heat-search key.

The Strawberry started to flash, and the screen was filled with swirls. It began to beep.

Flash! Bang! Crash!

"Oh, no! The Strawberry computer has crashed," said Rose.

"Oh, please think of something," Sonny begged. "I want to say sorry to Basil about hiding from him!"

"Who could help us to move these leaves?" said Rose.

The Superfairies all looked at each other.

"The Copper Queen!" they said at once.

Rose quickly flew to the Copper Courtyard at the end of the woods. The other Superfairies waited anxiously. It seemed to take forever for Rose to return.

Finally Rose reappeared. This time, the magnificent Copper Queen was by her side!

The Copper Queen was exceptionally beautiful. She had long, flowing hair, a magnifcent gown and cloak, and a berry-leaf crown.

"The Copper Queen is going to dance all the leaves away from here. Then we should be able to see the hole," said Rose.

"Hurrah!" everyone cried.

"Thank you, Copper Queen," said Star.

The Queen smiled but did not speak. She began to fly over the area where Basil was lost. Her movements grew faster and faster. As she danced in loops in the air, the leaves circled around her.

The Copper Queen moved behind the circles of leaves. With a great surge of power . . .

Puff! Whoosh! Shoo!

She blew them all away to another part of the woods.

The woodland floor was suddenly clear of leaves. In the middle of the clearing was the hole into which Basil had fallen.

"Thank you, Copper Queen!" said Rose. "Come on, Superfairies, there's no time to waste."

The Superfairies hovered over the hole. They could see Basil at the bottom, curled up in a ball.

"Basil, it's Rose," called the kind Superfairy.

Basil did not respond.

"Oh, no!" cried Sonny. "Is he going to be okay?"

"Yes, I think so," said Rose. "But the fall might have hurt his head and made him sleepy. I will blow him my healing kisses."

"It's dark in there," said Star. "Let me use my magic and do a dazzle so you can see."

"Three, two, one, prepare to dazzle," said Star.

Twinkle! Dazzle! Sparkle! Ta-da!

"Much brighter!" said Rose. "Thank you, Star!"

Rose floated down next to Basil and knelt beside him, blowing kisses.

Slowly, Basil began to open his eyes. "Oh, my head aches. Where am I?" he asked.

"It's okay, Basil," said Rose. "You fell down a hole in the woods, but you're all right now."

Berry hovered the fairycopter overhead. Silk spun a rescue silk and fastened it around Basil. They raised him to the safety of the fairycopter.

Star fixed a bandage around Basil's head. With the feather cloak around his shoulders, he felt much better.

"Thanks to the Copper Queen!" said Rose.

The Copper Queen smiled shyly. "I'm always happy to help," she said.

Chapter 4

# The Masked Dance

Later that day, the animals met the Superfairies by the cherry blossom tree. At last it was time for the Masked Dance!

Superfairy Rose looked pretty in a mask made from rose petals.

Superfairy Star looked shimmering in a mask made from gold leaves. Superfairy Berry wore a mask of rich, dark berries. Superfairy Silk's mask was fashioned from feathers.

The animals looked splendid too. They all wore beautiful masks, which made hide-and-seek very easy to play!

Susie, Martha and Violet held hands as they danced, enjoying their pretty masks.

"No one will know who we are!" said Martha.

"But we know who you are!" said Sonny. "You can't hide from us."

Basil, Sonny and Billy put on their masks too.

"We promise we won't play any tricks on you, Basil!" said Sonny.

"We'll never argue again," agreed Billy.

"I wasn't being fair," said Basil. "I should have shared with you. That's what friends

do. And I promise I won't boss you around again."

"Let's see how that goes!" Sonny said with a laugh. The three friends giggled and hugged.

A gentle wind *whooshed* through the woods at that moment.

"Here comes the Copper Queen!" called Susie, spotting the Queen in the distance.

The Copper Queen blushed a little as everyone admired her. She didn't like to be the star.

"She's gorgeous!" gasped Martha.

The Copper Queen danced all the way through the woods, bringing down the last of the leaves as she went. The Superfairies and all the animals danced behind her in their fancy masks.

They stopped at a roaring bonfire –
Crackle, Spark, Careful –

to toast marshmallows –
Splodge, Goo, Yum!

After that, it was time for a full feast. There was toasted nut-bread with butter and plum jam. There were pumpkin pies,

warming soups and yummy honey sponge pudding. There were delicious rhubarb and raspberry juices to wash it all down.

At the end of the Masked Dance, everyone was tired from dancing and had full tummies. Then they took turns singing songs.

"I don't want this to end!" said Susie Squirrel, even though it was way past her bedtime. She was exhausted from having so much autumn fun.

"I know!" agreed Violet. "We live in the best place in the whole world. I love how every season is so different."

"But autumn is especially beautiful," said Martha.

With a little nod of her head towards the Superfairies, the Copper Queen left the woods. As she disappeared, an amazing display of fireworks lit up the sky.

The Superfairies danced round the bonfire with all the animals looking on.

It had been a magnificent Masked Dance, and everyone had got along so well.

No bossing around at all. No tricks. And no accidents.

Everything in Peaseblossom Woods was just fine.

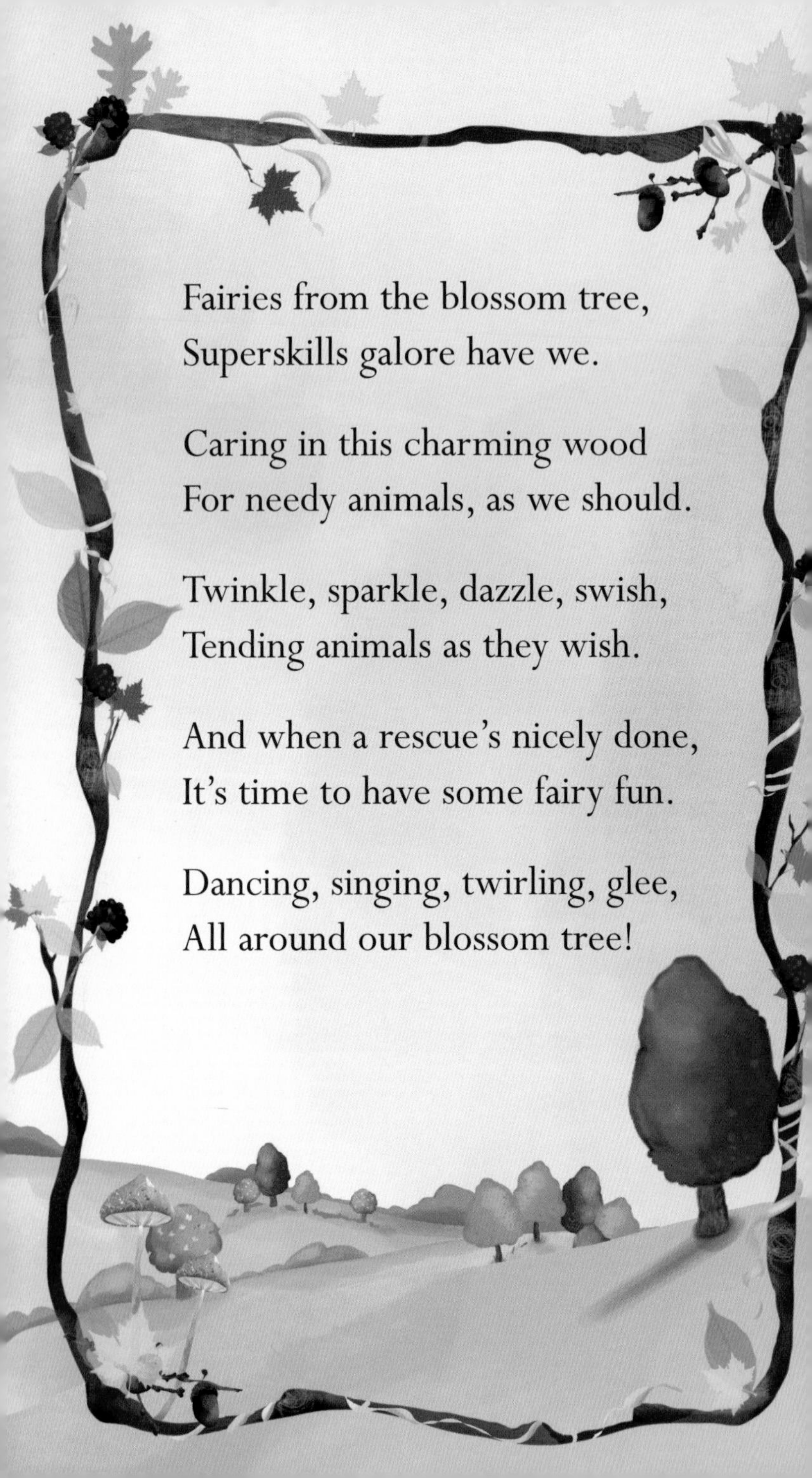

Fairies from the blossom tree,
Superskills galore have we.

Caring in this charming wood
For needy animals, as we should.

Twinkle, sparkle, dazzle, swish,
Tending animals as they wish.

And when a rescue's nicely done,
It's time to have some fairy fun.

Dancing, singing, twirling, glee,
All around our blossom tree!

# All about *fairies*

The legend of fairies is as old as time. Fairy tales tell stories of fairy magic. According to legend, fairies are so small and delicate, and fly so fast, that they might actually be all around us, but just very hard to see. Fairies, supposedly, only reveal themselves to believers.

Fairies often dance in circles at sunrise and sunset. They love to play in woodlands among wildflowers. If you sing gently to them, they may appear.

Here are some of the world's most famous fairies:

## The flower fairies

Artist Cicely Mary Barker painted a range of pretty flower fairies and published eight volumes of flower fairy art from 1923 onwards. The link between fairies and flowers is very strong.

She visits us during the night to leave a coin when we lose our baby teeth. Although it is very hard to catch sight of the tooth fairy, children are always happy when she visits.

## Fake fairies

In 1917, cousins Elsie Wright and Frances Griffiths said they had photographed fairies in their garden. They later admitted that most were fakes – but Frances claimed that one was genuine.

# Which Superfairy are you?

1. What is your favourite metal?
   - A) gold
   - B) silver
   - C) copper
   - D) bronze

2. What is your favourite breakfast?
   - A) cereal
   - B) toast
   - C) eggs
   - D) pancakes

3. Which is your least-favourite weather?
   - A) rain
   - B) snow
   - C) wind
   - D) cold

4. What material would you use to make a mask?
   - A) berries
   - B) feathers
   - C) gold leaves
   - D) petals

5. If you had a magic wand, would you . . .
   - A) feed everyone who is hungry
   - B) fly around the world
   - C) brighten up the world
   - D) make everyone who is ill feel better

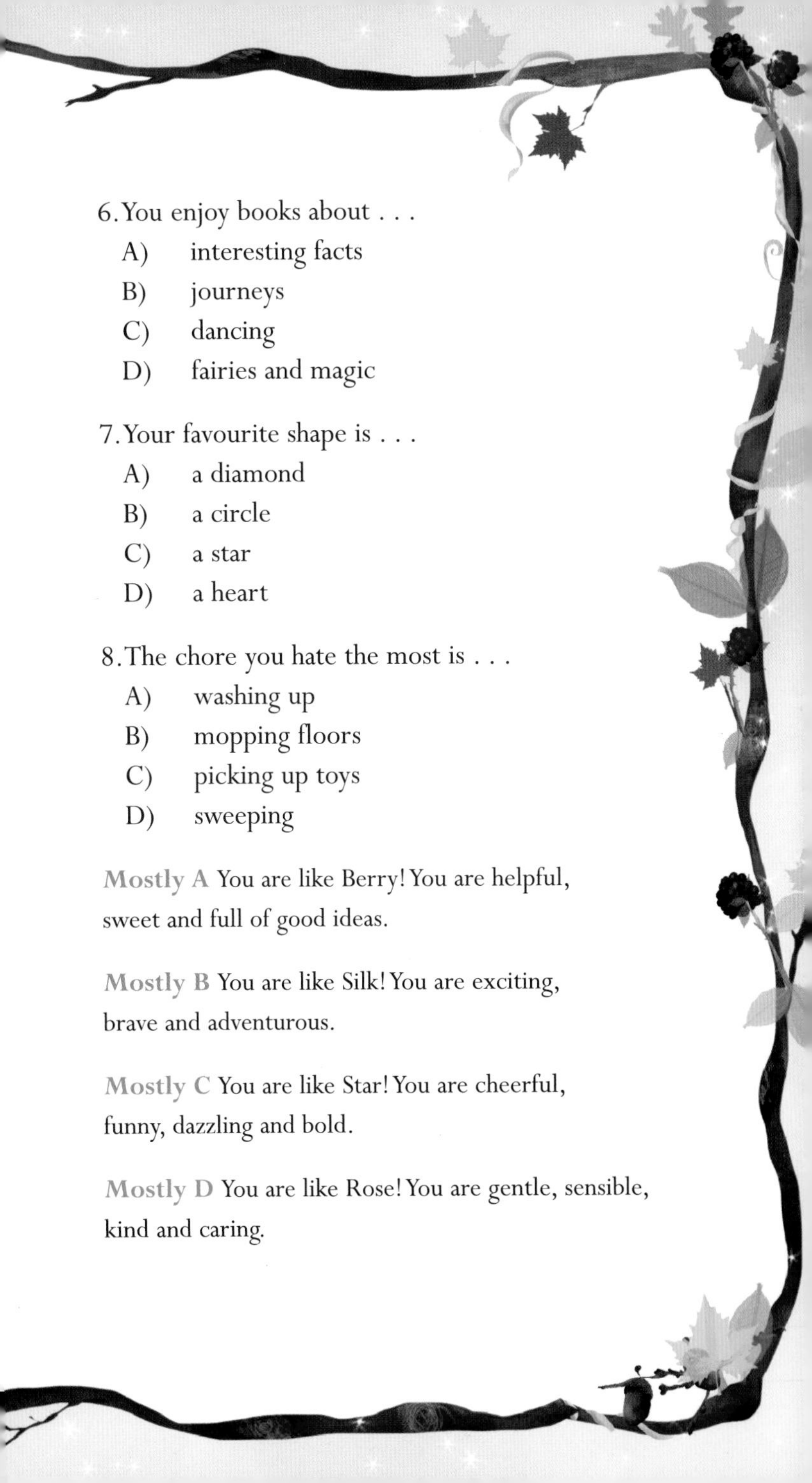

6. You enjoy books about . . .
   - A) interesting facts
   - B) journeys
   - C) dancing
   - D) fairies and magic

7. Your favourite shape is . . .
   - A) a diamond
   - B) a circle
   - C) a star
   - D) a heart

8. The chore you hate the most is . . .
   - A) washing up
   - B) mopping floors
   - C) picking up toys
   - D) sweeping

**Mostly A** You are like Berry! You are helpful, sweet and full of good ideas.

**Mostly B** You are like Silk! You are exciting, brave and adventurous.

**Mostly C** You are like Star! You are cheerful, funny, dazzling and bold.

**Mostly D** You are like Rose! You are gentle, sensible, kind and caring.

# About the author

Janey Louise Jones has been a published author for ten years. Her Princess Poppy series is an international bestselling brand, with books translated into ten languages, including Hebrew and Mandarin. Janey is a graduate of Edinburgh University and lives in Edinburgh, Scotland, with her three sons. She loves fairies, princesses, beaches and woodlands.

# About the illustrator

Jennie Poh was born in England and grew up in Malaysia (in the jungle). At the age of ten, she moved back to England and trained as a ballet dancer. She studied fine art at Surrey Institute of Art & Design as well as fashion illustration at Central Saint Martins. Jennie loves the countryside, animals, tea and reading. She lives in Woking, England, with her husband and two wonderful daughters.

# THE *Fun* DOESN'T STOP HERE!

JOIN THE SUPERFAIRIES ON MORE MAGICAL ANIMAL RESCUES!

Superfairies
Basil the Bear Cub
by Janey Louise Jones

Superfairies
Dancer the Wild Pony
by Janey Louise Jones

Superfairies
Martha the Little Mouse
by Janey Louise Jones

Superfairies
Violet the Velvet Rabbit
by Janey Louise Jones

Superfairies
Sonny the Daring Squirrel
by Janey Louise Jones

Superfairies
Farrah the Shy Fawn
by Janey Louise Jones

For more exciting books *from*
brilliant authors, *follow* the *fox*!

www.curious-fox.com